Pocket
·Cats·

Paw Power

A DAVID FICKLING BOOK

Published in the United States by David Fickling Books,
an imprint of Random House Children's Books,
a division of Random House, Inc., New York.
Originally published in Great Britain by David Fickling Books,
an imprint of Random House Children's Books,
a division of the Random House Group Ltd., London, in 2010.

David Fickling Books and the colophon are trademarks of David Fickling.

Visit us on the Web!
www.randomhouse.com/kids

Educators and librarians, for a variety of teaching tools, visit us at
www.randomhouse.com/teachers

Library of Congress Cataloging-in-Publication Data
Wells, Kitty.
Paw power / Kitty Wells ; [illustrations by Joanna Harrison].
p.   cm. — (Pocket cats)
Summary: After Maddy buys a set of three ceramic cats at a mysterious
flea market stall, one of the statues comes to life to help her stop a school bully.
ISBN 978-0-385-75201-5 (trade) — ISBN 978-0-385-75202-2 (lib. bdg.) —
ISBN 978-0-375-89567-8 (ebook)
[1. Cats—Fiction. 2. Magic—Fiction. 3. Bullies—Fiction. 4. Schools—Fiction.]
I. Harrison, Joanna, ill. II. Title.
PZ7.W46485Paw 2011
[Fic]—dc22
2010011892

Printed in the United States of America
January 2011
10 9 8 7 6 5 4 3 2 1

First American Edition

Pocket ·Cats·

Paw Power

Kitty Wells

illustrated by Joanna Harrison

David Fickling Books

OXFORD · NEW YORK

The *Pocket Cats* series is dedicated to all cat lovers, everywhere . . . including you!

Chapter One

Maddy carefully licked the last of the ice cream off her spoon, and glanced at her mother. Was now a good time to ask? She had been waiting for the perfect moment all day, but so far none had presented itself – not at the aquarium, or the toy store, or the zoo.

Now her mum had the map of London attractions spread out over the café table, with Maddy's little

1

brother, Jack, peering over her elbow.

"Let's do the London Dungeon!" he cried, pointing.

"I don't think we'll have time before our train," said Mum, peering at her watch. She folded up the map and tucked it away in her bag. "How about a nice stroll through Hyde Park? Maddy?"

"Great!" exclaimed Maddy, bouncing on her seat as Jack groaned. A stroll through the park – perfect! Jack would be running around like he always did, and she'd have Mum all to herself. She could ask her then.

At first it seemed like Maddy's plan would work. She waited until they were standing on a bridge over a stream, with Jack racing back and forth playing Pooh Sticks. Mum was leaning against the railing, smiling at the ducks.

Maddy cleared her throat. "Mum?" she said casually.

"What, sweetie?" said her mother.

Maddy took a deep breath. "Well . . . Polly – that's a girl in my ballet class – she has a cat called Fanta, and Fanta's just had kittens, and *everyone* wants one, but Polly says I can have first pick once they're old enough! Isn't that great?"

3

"Oh, Maddy—" started her mother.

Maddy kept on in a rush, her voice pleading: "She says I can *have* it, Mum, so it won't cost anything at all. There's three boys and two girls, and they're all ginger, and Polly says they're so, so cute! Which would you rather have, a boy or a girl?" She looked hopefully at her mother.

Mum shook her head. "Maddy, you *know* you can't have a cat. Jack is allergic, remember?"

Maddy had expected this. Her voice rose as she talked faster. "Yes, but – Mum, listen – Polly says that her dad's allergic too, but he takes a special pill and then he's fine! She's going to find out what it is and tell me so that Jack can take it too, and—"

"Maddy, *no*." Her mother brushed a

4

strand of brown hair out of her eyes.
"Jack's allergies are more serious than
that. He has asthma, and cat fur makes
it worse. Pills won't help."

"But—"

"*No.* That's final."

When her mother said something
was final, she meant it. Hot, babyish
tears pricked at Maddy's eyes. She
had been so sure that she could have
a kitten! She had already decided on
one of the girls. She'd been going to

call it Marmalade, and let it sleep at the bottom of her bed.

"I'm sorry, love," said her mum gently. "I know how much you want a cat."

"It's not fair," muttered Maddy, staring down at her feet. "Jack has his stupid hamsters."

"You could have a hamster too, if you wanted."

Maddy made a face. She liked most

animals, but she couldn't warm to hamsters. All they did was gallop about pointlessly on their wheel, or sleep in piles of sawdust.

Paw Power

Jack drifted over, rattling a stick against the bridge's railings. "What's with you?" he asked Maddy, seeing her expression.

"Nothing," snapped Maddy, wiping her eyes.

"Maddy was hoping to get a kitten," their mother explained. "So she's a bit disappointed."

"You *can't* have a kitten. I'm allergic," said Jack importantly.

"Yes, I know!" shouted Maddy.

She turned and ran blindly over the bridge, her trainers slapping the tarmac. Her mother joined her without a word, taking her hand. With Jack holding her other hand, they walked through the rest of the park and out into the London streets.

Maddy trudged along in a daze of

disappointment. In her imagination, she and Marmalade had been the best of friends for ages. Now Marmalade would go to some other girl, and be called something else entirely. The unfairness of it ached in Maddy's chest.

"Oh, look," said her mother, pausing at the gates of a small square. "There's an antique market going on. Shall we have a quick wander? We've still got time."

Maddy shrugged listlessly. The

market was full of brightly coloured
stands, but she couldn't have been
less interested in them at the moment.
Jack didn't look keen either.

"Boring!" he moaned, tugging at
Mum's hand. "London Dungeon,
Mum, come on."

"Just a quick look," she said,
steering them inside. "Two ticks, I
promise."

Maddy and Jack grimaced at
each other. Mum was mad about
antiques; they'd probably never get
her out.

Maddy trailed along after her
mother and Jack as they went from
stall to stall. The market had lots
of different ones, for such a little
square. There were antique stamps,
and postcards, and old-fashioned

9

jewellery. One stand even had antique taps for your sink.

Suddenly Maddy froze. There was a large blonde girl standing nearby with her parents, looking at old-fashioned toys. Though the girl was half turned away, Maddy could see her look of boredom, and the slight sneer curling her lip.

Sherry Newton!

Maddy's heart felt like it had dropped to the cobbled ground. She quickly turned away, flipping through a box of antique postcards without noticing them. What was Sherry doing *here*?

The girl and her parents moved closer. Maddy swung her long brown hair in front of her face, trying to hide behind it. Finding a classmate

10

at an *antique market* was just the
sort of thing Sherry and her friends
might torment you with for weeks to
come!

Yawning, Sherry looked right at her.
Maddy winced. Now the sharp blue
eyes would narrow, and an evil smile
would spread across Sherry's face—

Suddenly Maddy sagged in relief.
The girl wasn't Sherry at all. She was
older, and her blue eyes were mild.

11

She gave Maddy an uninterested look, and turned back to her parents.

Maddy's heart felt heavy as she pushed the postcards back into place. She was such a coward. Sherry Newton hardly even noticed Maddy at school, yet here she was seeing the class bully when she wasn't even there!

It was probably a good thing for Marmalade that the little cat would be going to someone else.

Jack came darting back. "I've found something for you!"

"What?" asked Maddy dully.

"Come and see!"

He dragged Maddy over to a stall she hadn't noticed, in the corner of the square. Its awning cast a dark shadow over the mishmash of trinkets spread out across a dusty purple cloth.

"Look – cats!" he crowed. "And these ones won't make me sneeze."

Maddy scowled. Jack was pointing to a set of small ceramic cats. "Oh, ha, ha," she said.

Dodging her shove, Jack danced back to Mum, giggling. Maddy sighed as she looked at the cats. There were three of them, nestled neatly together like puzzle pieces, tails and paws entwined.

Chapter One

As if she'd want *fake* cats! What
was the point of that? But even so,
Maddy found herself reaching for
them, all thoughts of Sherry forgotten.

"What is your business?" intoned a
deep voice.

Maddy started. From the shadowy
depths of the stall a woman had
appeared. She was swathed in gauzy
purple robes that had tiny clinking
coins on them, like a belly dancer's
skirt. Her hair was a deep blue-
black shot with streaks of purest
silver, and tumbled down past her
shoulders.

"I – I just wanted to look at the
cats," gasped Maddy. She glanced
around quickly, and was reassured to
see her mother standing a few stalls
away, looking at copper pots.

Paw Power

The woman smiled, showing a gold tooth. "Ah, the cats . . . of course." Plucking them up from between a set of old spoons and something that looked like a shark's tooth, she handed them to Maddy.

Maddy examined them curiously. What a clever little set! There was a small black cat, a grey one, and a long-haired tabby with white markings. All at once her pulse quickened.

Where the cats' tails came together, they formed two curly letters:

Maddy gaped. *ML!* Those were *her* initials: Maddy Lloyd. Looking more closely, she could see that the

15

way the tails wound together was just
a coincidence. Turned another way,
they looked like a "W". But still . . .

She regarded the cats in wonder.
They nestled in her palm as if they
were meant to be there.

"You have seen something,
perhaps?" purred the woman. Her
green eyes glinted.

"Could I buy these?" blurted
Maddy.

"Perhaps, perhaps
not," said the
woman, narrowing
her gaze.

Maddy blinked.
"Um – well, I've
been saving up
my pocket money,
so I've got ten
pounds—"

17

The woman's long earrings jangled as she shook her head. "It is not a question of money. Give me your palm."

Before Maddy quite knew what was happening, the woman had grabbed her free hand and started tracing its lines with a long pointed nail. Maddy gulped as the scent of exotic spices tickled her nose. The woman's hands looked older than the rest of her,

somehow, with silver rings crowding every finger.

"You are nine years old," she announced, staring down at Maddy's palm. "And you take ballet. You have always wanted a cat, and you wish to save the tigers in India when you are older."

Maddy's mouth fell open. She'd been worried about the world's tigers ever since her father told her they were near extinction – but she hadn't told *anybody* that, not even her best friend Rachel!

"Um – yes," she squeaked. She saw with relief that her mother was now only two stalls away.

The woman dropped Maddy's hand, inspecting her closely. "Blue eyes, freckles . . . you are small for your

19

Chapter One

age. And you think you are a coward."
She chuckled.

Hot shame swept over Maddy as
she thought of the girl who hadn't
been Sherry. "Um – is ten pounds
enough?" she whispered, her cheeks
burning. She fumbled in the pocket of
her jeans. "I've got it right here."

The woman smiled. "No, my dear.
Ten pounds is not enough."

"Oh." Maddy held the note limply.

"They have chosen you, I can see

that," continued the woman, nodding at the cats. "So the question is – what will you give for them that is of worth?"

Maddy started to say that she didn't know what the woman meant – but then all at once she *did* know. Setting the cats down carefully on the purple cloth, she delved into her pocket again.

"Here," she said, her heart thumping as she placed a coin with a star on it onto the counter. "It was my grandfather's – he carried it all through the war. He said it was his lucky piece."

Maddy felt a sharp pang as the woman picked up the coin and turned it this way and

21

that. Her grandfather's lucky piece! But she knew, instinctively, that this would be a fair trade.

The woman nodded in satisfaction, and tucked the coin away in her jingling robes. "A *falus* from Morocco. Very apt. They have seen Morocco many times, haven't you, my loves?"

Maddy realized with a start that she was talking to the cats! Before she could react, the woman had scooped them up and started wrapping them in tissue paper.

Suddenly Maddy's mother appeared. "What have you been buying, then?" she asked, squeezing Maddy's shoulder.

"Just . . . a set of ceramic cats," said Maddy guiltily. She could never tell her mother that she'd given away Grandpa's lucky coin.

Mum smiled sympathetically. "Ceramic, eh? Good, no one's allergic to that."

"She has excellent taste," said the woman cheerfully, popping the cats in a paper bag. Suddenly she looked much more ordinary; not startling at all. Maddy stared. Had she only imagined the oddness of the encounter?

Chapter One

Her mother moved on to the next stall, where Jack was busy pawing through a box of lead soldiers. The woman handed the paper bag to Maddy, who took it gratefully – but as she tried to draw her hand away, the woman grabbed her wrist with bony fingers.

"You must greet them properly before you've had them twenty-four hours," she hissed, her green eyes blazing like jungle fire. "Do not forget!"

Chapter Two

On the train journey home Maddy sat with the paper bag on her lap, her thoughts tumbling wildly. What had the woman meant – that the cats had "chosen" Maddy? She'd acted as if they could understand what she was saying!

She must have been a bit mad, Maddy decided. Even so, she felt uneasy about the whole thing, and was relieved when her mother suggested a word game to pass the time.

When the train finally pulled into their station, Maddy's mother stretched. "Oh, it's been a lovely day out," she said. "Do you suppose your father's burned our tea?"

"Yeah, he's nuked it!" shouted Jack.

Maddy followed them off the train, clutching her paper bag. The episode in the antique market seemed almost like a dream now. She could hardly remember why she'd wanted the cats so much. They were only ceramic figures!

What had she been thinking of, giving away her grandfather's coin?

Paw Power

★

All that evening, the paper bag sat on Maddy's desk like a guilty conscience. Finally, before she went to bed that night, she slowly opened it and unwound the tissue-wrapped package.

The three cats tumbled neatly into her palm. Sliding into her desk chair, Maddy experimented with fitting them together and taking them apart again. Their bodies felt cool and smooth, and made tiny *clinking* noises.

Her spirits lifted a bit. They really *were* a lovely set – and the curly *ML* formed by their tails was as clear as before. Turning on her desk light, Maddy inspected the cats one by one.

The grey cat was the largest. Its ceramic body was comfortably chunky: just the type of cat she'd

love to pick up
and cuddle, if it
were real. It had
bluish-grey fur,
and golden eyes that
looked friendly.

"You're nice, aren't
you?" murmured Maddy,
stroking his grey head. Placing him
gently back on her desk, she picked
up the black cat.

It was the smallest of the three:

a slender piece
of midnight with
bright green eyes.
Its inky face had a
veiled expression
that seemed to
stare right back at
Maddy.

Paw Power

It's a cat that has secrets, thought Maddy. The idea pleased her. Cats *should* have secrets; it's the sort of creatures they were.

Last, she picked up the long-haired tabby. Its face was a startled white mask over stripy brown markings, with dancing amber eyes. This cat looked like it had secrets too – but funny ones that it would share with you, if you asked. Maddy found herself smiling as she looked at it.

Suddenly remembering what the woman had said, she lined up the three cats in a neat row, facing her. She wasn't

exactly sure what "greeting the cats" meant, but the woman had been so insistent that Maddy thought she'd better do it.

She took a deep breath. "Um . . . greetings," she said shyly.

The cats' painted eyes watched her. *Go on*, they seemed to be saying.

"Greetings," repeated Maddy, more confidently this time. "I mean, hello! My name is Maddy – Madeleine Lloyd."

She stood up and bowed. Then, because she wasn't certain whether a bow was the right thing when you were a girl (or when you were talking to cats), she attempted a curtsy as well. She was rather good at this because of her ballet lessons, though her nightdress didn't have the right

sort of skirt, and spoiled the effect a
bit.

Something else still seemed to be
needed. Maddy thought for a moment,
and then touched each cat briefly
on its smooth head. "I'm very, very
pleased to meet you," she said.

A strong, waiting silence seemed to
take root and grow. It wrapped about
the room, encircling Maddy and the

cats. All at once there were hundreds
of butterflies in her stomach. She
stared at the cats, not daring to move.

Nothing happened.

Maddy let out a breath. Well, what
had she expected? Suddenly she
 started giggling, and
couldn't stop. What
would her best friend
Rachel say, when
Maddy told her that she
had curtsied to a bunch
of ceramic cats?

Still smiling, she climbed into bed
and switched off the light.

The touch on her cheek was as light as
thistledown, tapping her over and over.
Maddy shook her head in her sleep.
The touch paused, and then continued.

Paw Power

Tap, tap. Tap. Tap, tap.

"Mm?" she muttered drowsily.

Tap, tap, tap.

Still half asleep, Maddy brushed her hand across her face . . . and felt something soft.

She jolted awake with a shriek, lunging for her bedside lamp. A moth! A great big horrible moth was flapping about her room! At the same moment a grey streak leaped from her pillow to her bedside table, landing with a small, solid *thump.*

"Easy," said a calm voice. "You'll wake the whole house, carrying on like that."

Maddy gasped. Sitting beside her ballerina lamp was the grey cat from her new set. He blinked at her and gave a friendly purr.

33

"Better now?" he enquired politely.

He was completely and unquestionably alive . . . and only five centimetres tall. Maddy gaped at him, unable to move.

"What's wrong?" he asked. "Cat got your tongue?" He chuckled at his own joke.

Paw Power

"You – you're *real*," whispered Maddy. She pinched herself under the bedclothes, and winced.

The cat looked affronted. "Naturally I'm real. Why shouldn't I be?"

There were so many answers to this that Maddy didn't know where to begin. Her gaze flew to the other cats. They still sat on the desk where she'd left them.

The grey cat gave a long stretch, pulling his body to its full length. "Ah, that's better!" he purred. "One does get a bit stiff, sitting in the same position for so long."

Suddenly he leaped onto the bed, landing

beside the mound that was Maddy's leg. The pink and white duvet plumped up around him, and he scrambled onto her knee. "May I?" he asked, nodding at her hand.

Hardly daring to breathe, Maddy held out her hand. The cat stepped delicately onto it, settling himself in the centre of her palm. She could feel the warm *aliveness* of him, the small but definite weight.

Carefully she raised her hand until the cat was almost at eye-level. Oh, he was beautiful! A miniature, perfect cat with golden eyes, and the most strokable-looking fur she had ever seen.

"Do you have a name?" she asked softly.

The cat twitched his tail, looking

amused. "Of course I have a name.
It's Greykin."

"Greykin," murmured Maddy,
enchanted. She longed to run a finger
across his gleaming bluish-grey fur,
but was too shy to ask. Remembering
her manners, she sat up straighter.
"I'm pleased to meet you, Greykin.
I'm—"

"I already know who you are,"
interrupted Greykin gently. "You

greeted us earlier, Maddy Lloyd.
That's what brought me to life."

Maddy's mouth dropped open. So
the woman hadn't been mad after
all!

Greykin looked at her desk. "Would
you take me back to my compatriots
for a moment?"

Maddy blinked, and then realized he
meant the other cats. She slithered out
of bed, holding Greykin as steadily as
she could. Carrying him to her desk,
she laid her hand flat, and he stepped
off her palm as neatly as getting out
of a lift.

Sliding onto her desk chair, Maddy
watched, wide-eyed, as Greykin
padded first to the black cat and then
the tabby, solemnly touching noses
with both. She half expected the other

38

two to burst into life as well, but their painted features remained cold and silent.

Coming back towards Maddy, Greykin sat beside her pencil case. They were just the same height. "Would you mind putting them together?" he asked. "It makes their job easier."

"What job?" asked Maddy softly. With a tiny *clink*, she arranged the two cats so that they were entwined once more.

"That's better," said Greykin. "The job of keeping me alive, of course." He smiled at her bewildered expression. "Shall I explain?"

"Yes, *please*," said Maddy. "Only – only first . . ." She hesitated, biting her lip.

39

Paw Power

"What is it?" asked Greykin.

"Oh, *could* I stroke you?" Maddy burst out in a whisper. "I've just been dying to – your fur looks so soft!"

Greykin's furry face beamed. "Of course you may," he said. "It *is* rather soft, if I say so myself."

Holding her breath, Maddy slowly ran her index finger down his back. It was even softer than she'd imagined, like stroking rich velvet!

A low rumbling filled the air as Greykin purred. "You may do that again, if you like," he said dreamily. "Perhaps with a bit of fingernail this time?"

Maddy scratched his back – tentatively at first, and then harder as the grey cat hummed with pleasure, butting his head against her hand.

She could feel the tiny tickle of his whiskers, and giggled.

At last Greykin sat back on his haunches with a contented sigh.

"Very nice; thank you. It's been a good fifty years or so since I was last scratched."

Maddy gaped at him. "Fifty *years*?"

Greykin nodded. "Yes. We don't bond easily, or often. It has to be the right sort of human who greets us before we can wake – though we do sometimes help things along with a bit of a hint." His grey tail coiled into an L.

"My initials!" breathed Maddy.

42

Paw Power

"You really *were* meant for me."

"Indeed." Greykin smiled. Flicking his ears towards the other two cats, he added, "You see, they're working very hard right now – providing the *ka* that I need. It helps if they're touching each other."

"What's *ka*?" asked Maddy eagerly.

The cat cocked his round face to one side as he considered. "Life force. Energy. Magic. It's what makes us able to come to life."

Maddy looked again at the black cat and the tabby.

"Yes, they can come awake as well," said Greykin, answering her unspoken question. "But only one of us

at a time can ever do so. It takes a lot of *ka* from the other two, you see."

"What are their names?" asked Maddy. She started to touch the tabby's head, and then drew her finger away. It seemed disrespectful somehow, now that she knew these two could come alive too.

Greykin settled down beside the pencil case, tucking his paws under his chunky body. "Their names are their own to tell – you'll meet them sometime in the future, when it's their turn. But for now, it's I who have been chosen for the task ahead."

"Task?" echoed Maddy. The cat's golden eyes gazed at her, unblinking. Her pulse quickened. "What do you mean?"

Greykin leaped to where Maddy's

hand lay on the desk and curled his tail around her little finger. "It's very simple," he said. "We've a job to do together, you and I."

Chapter Three

W hen Maddy woke up the next
morning she lay in bed for
a moment, trying to remember the
wonderful dream she'd had. There
had been something soft . . . a pair of
golden eyes . . . and magic, the most
amazing magic!

It came back in a rush. Maddy
scrambled out of bed and darted over
to her desk. The three ceramic cats sat
clustered together, stiff and smooth.

The grey one's painted eyes stared
blankly at her.

"Oh," murmured Maddy. She
dropped onto her chair. A dream. It
had only been a dream.

Hot tears clutched her throat.
Slowly she disentangled Greykin and
held him on her palm. It had been
babyish to believe in magic, even for
a moment, but – but this had seemed
so *real*! He had sat on her hand, he
had talked! He—

Paw Power

She froze as a ripple ran across the grey cat's surface. Painted ceramic melted away into warm, living fur.

The cat sat up, blinking pleasantly. "Good morning," he said.

"Arghh!" shrieked Maddy. She jerked her hand back, and then shrieked again as Greykin clung to hold on, digging his claws into her palm.

"Careful, I'll fall off!" he yowled.

"Maddy?" called Maddy's mother.
"Are you all right?"

"Fine!" gasped Maddy over her
shoulder. "Let *go*, that hurts!" she
hissed at Greykin. Tiny red dots
welled up on her palm as the cat
retracted his claws, watching her warily.

"*You* all right!" he huffed. "What
about *me*, I'd like to know?" He
leaped onto the desk and turned his
tiny back on her, lashing his tail.

Maddy's heart thudded. He was
alive! He really was!

Maddy's mum poked her head in.
"What was that shouting about?"

"I . . ." Maddy glanced wildly at
Greykin. He was ceramic once more,
frozen safely in place. "I thought I
saw . . . a moth."

50

Paw Power

Her mother rolled her eyes. "You and your moths. Come on, it's almost time for breakfast."

The door shut again. Maddy waited for her mum's footsteps to fade away, and then lunged across the desk. "It's all right, she's gone," she whispered urgently. *"Please*, change back!"

Slowly Greykin's soft fur returned. He peered coldly over his shoulder. "Well? Are you going to screech in horror and try to fling me across the room again?"

Maddy winced. "I'm sorry. It's just – I thought last night was a dream. I couldn't believe it when you were really real!"

"Mmm," sniffed Greykin. "Yes, you registered your surprise quite effectively." But he seemed a bit less cross, and turned to face her. "Did I hear someone mention breakfast?"

Maddy straightened. "Oh! Are you hungry? I mean – do you eat?"

"I don't *have* to, but it's a very pleasant pastime," said Greykin. "I particularly enjoy a nice bit of bacon." He looked at her pointedly.

"I'll go and get you some right now!" said Maddy. Quickly she pulled on a pair of jeans and a bright red sweatshirt with pockets. She felt like singing. Greykin was real, he really was!

"*You'll* go?" Greykin shook his furry head. "*I'll* go with you, you mean."

Maddy was crawling about on the

52

Paw Power

floor, looking for her stripy socks. She glanced up in alarm. "But you can't go downstairs; they'd see you!" She knew without question that this would be simply awful. Her parents were very nice people, but they would never understand about a magical cat only five centimetres tall.

Greykin's expression was suddenly serious. He leaped up onto her stapler and flicked his tail at her. "Don't you

remember what we talked about last night? I must see the rest of the house; it's very important."

Maddy's sock dangled from her hand as she stared at him. In the excitement of realizing that Greykin was real, she *had* forgotten what he'd said the night before. Suddenly it all flew back to her.

According to Greykin, he and the other cats only came to life when there was a problem that needed solving. Their duty was to fix whatever was wrong – and they needed her help to do it. But first they had to find out what the problem was.

Last night this had seemed exciting and magical. Now, in the cold light of day, Maddy felt a twist of worry in her stomach.

54

Paw Power

"Er . . . what sort of problem do you think it might be?" she asked nervously, pulling on her sock. "It won't be anything dangerous, will it?"

Greykin shrugged. "Sometimes there's danger. And sometimes it's only a small problem, though very important to the person involved. Other times, of course, it's not a person at all."

"What then?" Maddy frowned.

"Oh, all sorts of things." Greykin's broad, furry face squinted in remembrance. "Once, in India, we had to save an ancient tree from a colony of termites. Millions of them – fat white things over two centimetres long."

"Urgh!" Maddy drew back in disgust.

Greykin chuckled, and hopped down onto her desk. "I don't imagine we'll have that problem here," he said kindly. "But I need to feel the rest of the house before I'll know anything – and that's why I *must* go downstairs with you. One of your pockets will do nicely," he added, looking at her sweatshirt.

"My . . ." Maddy glanced down, and grinned. Oh, of course! She could

56

take him downstairs after all. Smiling widely, she went over to the desk and held out her hand. Greykin stepped onto her palm again, and she tucked the little cat into her pocket.

"Are you OK?" she asked, peering in.

"Very comfortable," replied Greykin, curling into a warm grey ball.

Maddy couldn't resist giving his
fur a quick stroke, and he touched
his nose to her finger in a friendly
way. A sudden giggle escaped her at
the thought of eating breakfast with
Greykin in her pocket – and the rest
of her family not having a clue!

"Maddy, this is a serious matter,
you know," chided Greykin's
muffled voice from the depths of her
sweatshirt. "And please don't forget
the bacon."

At breakfast, Maddy cut off small
pieces of bacon and smuggled them
down to Greykin, trying not to laugh
as she felt the little cat moving about.

Her father winked at her from
across the table. "You've got ants in
your pants this morning, haven't you?"

"Ants in her knickers!" said Jack, sniggering into his orange juice.

Maddy bit the inside of her lip to keep from bursting into wild laughter. "No – not ants," she choked out. But she tried to settle down after that, in case her family got suspicious.

After breakfast Maddy wandered about the house so that Greykin could "feel" every room. He'd been very firm about the need for this. Worry began knotting Maddy's stomach again as she circled upstairs and down.

What if the problem was something awful? Was her family in some sort of trouble? Everyone *seemed* all right – Jack was playing with his hamsters, and her dad was in his study working on his book – but how could she tell?

Paw Power

"Maddy, go
and watch a DVD
or something!"
exclaimed her
mother finally,
looking up from
the computer.
"You're making
me nervous,
pacing about like that."

"Sorry," muttered Maddy.
Returning to her room, she closed the
door and placed Greykin on her chest
of drawers. "Did you find it?" she
asked anxiously, keeping her voice
low in case Jack was listening. He
was a terrible snoop.

"It's not here," announced Greykin.
He prowled across the white
painted top of her chest of drawers,

61

examining each item with interest.

"Are you sure? How do you know?"

"Simple." He stopped to sniff at a plastic bangle that was larger than he was. "When I find what needs to be done, my whiskers tingle. My whiskers haven't tingled once in your house. So I deduce, it's somewhere else."

Phew! Maddy's shoulders slumped with relief.

Greykin reached her ballerina jewellery box and stood on his hind legs, peering in and swishing his tail. Oh, he was just the most perfect little cat! Maddy hugged herself, still hardly able to believe that this was real.

All at once Greykin leaped into the box. "This will do nicely, once you clear away all the clutter."

Maddy blinked. "Nicely for what?"

He peered up at her with his golden eyes. "A bed for me, of course. It needs to be someplace hidden, or else I have to turn back to ceramic at night."

Charmed by the idea, Maddy scooped out a string of plastic beads and a small locket, placing them on her chest of drawers. Then she frowned. "But, Greykin . . . if the problem's not here, then where *is* it?"

"All I know is that it will be someplace connected with you. Where else do you go?" Greykin nosed at a hair-scrunchy. "That can stay; it looks rather comfortable."

Maddy found a few more scrunchies and made him a cosy nest as she

thought. "Well . . . school, mostly," she said. "And ballet class twice a week. And we go swimming at the sports centre sometimes," she added.

Greykin shuddered. "Water? No thank you! We'll start with school."

Maddy's hand froze. "But—"

A hundred thoughts crashed together in her mind. She could show Greykin to Rachel! Her best friend would be utterly gobsmacked. But what if Mrs Pratt, Maddy's teacher, saw him? Or *Sherry Newton*?

"What's wrong?" asked Greykin. He leaped onto her wrist and bounded nimbly up to her shoulder, barely larger than a mouse. His soft fur tickled Maddy's neck as he nuzzled her.

"Um . . . nothing." Maddy tried to

smile. She *couldn't* let Greykin know what a coward she was; it was too embarrassing. "OK, you can come to school with me – but we'll have to make *very* sure you keep out of sight!"

Chapter Four

When Maddy got to school on Monday morning, her best friend Rachel came racing across the playground, all long legs and flying blonde hair.

"Did you ask your mum about the kitten?" she asked breathlessly, straightening her glasses.

Maddy blinked. She'd forgotten all about the kitten! "Yes, but she said no," she said. "But, Rachel, listen,

you'll never believe it – the most
incredible thing has happened!" She
drew her friend over to the swings,
and plunged into her story.

"Very funny," grinned Rachel. She
twirled round on the swing. "You
should write that down in a story."

"But I'm not joking," said Maddy in
surprise. It hadn't occurred to her that
her friend wouldn't believe her.

Rachel raised her eyebrows
sceptically. "Maddy, it's a bit early for
April Fool's Day. It's only October!"

Maddy glanced around. Sherry
Newton and her gang were safely
across the yard, clustered around
a DS. "You cheated!" Maddy heard
Sherry shout angrily, shoving one of
her friends. "*I* should have won that
one!"

Chapter Four

"I brought him with me," said
Maddy in a low voice.

Rachel's blue eyes widened. She
scuffed at the ground to stop her
swinging. "What – really?"

"Really. But, Rachel, you can't
tell *anyone*." Maddy hopped off the
swing and picked up her school
bag. She stared solemnly into
Rachel's eyes. "OK? It's very, very
important."

Rachel slid off her swing too,
frowning in confusion. "Well – of
course I won't – but Maddy, it's not
real, is it? I mean, it can't be!"

Maddy unzipped her bag and took
out her flowered pencil case. Greykin
had been a bit huffy at the idea of
travelling in the case, and had only
agreed once she'd made him a little

bed inside, with scraps of bacon in case he got hungry.

"Are you ready?" she whispered.

"Er – I suppose." Rachel's eyes were bulging. She edged closer to Maddy, staring down at the case as if a snake might slither out of it.

"Greykin, this is my best friend, Rachel," said Maddy. She eased open the zip, taking care not to startle him. Peering inside, her heart sank. A small grey ceramic cat sat in the case.

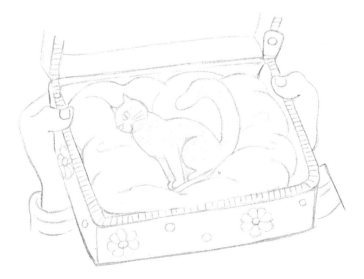

Rachel burst out laughing. "Maddy, you loon! You really had me going!"

"*Greykin*," hissed Maddy, cheeks flaming. She poked at the figurine. "Greykin, you have to change now!"

"All right, Mad, joke over." Still giggling, Rachel wiped her eyes.

"Greykin, *please*," begged Maddy, rattling the case. The cat remained cold and silent. He had already eaten all the bacon too, she noticed – the greedy thing!

Rachel was looking at her strangely. "Maddy . . . it's only a toy."

"He is *not* a toy," snapped Maddy, closing the case and putting it back into her bag. Even if what she was saying was incredible, her best friend should still believe her.

"Fine, whatever," said Rachel with

a groan. "Come on, we'd better get inside."

Maddy kept her pencil case on her desk all through the morning lessons, craning to hear any sign of movement. But the flowered case remained silent, and whenever she peeked inside, Greykin was still ceramic.

Was it someone in their class who was in trouble? Maddy's gaze fell on a large girl with dark blonde hair and freckles, and she shivered.

Sherry Newton's speciality was *causing* trouble, not being in it. She ruled over 5A along with her two friends, a pair of sneering red-haired

girls who were both called Jo. Jo
Pearson had short, spiky hair and Jo
Perkins had a pointy face, but apart
from that Maddy could barely tell
them apart. They both fawned over
Sherry, and backed her up in whatever
nastiness she came up with.

"Maddy! Stop daydreaming and
get to work," barked Mrs Pratt.
Maddy jumped, and returned to her
maths paper.

When the bell rang for lunch, she
hung back uncertainly. She couldn't
leave Greykin here – what if he
came to life while she was gone?
But if she took her pencil case to
lunch, people might start to wonder
what was inside. People like Sherry,
for instance. On impulse, Maddy
unzipped the pencil case and slipped

Paw Power

Greykin into her pocket.

"Hurry up, Maddy!" called Mrs
Pratt, clapping her hands. "We're all
ready to go."

"What's with you today?"
whispered Rachel as 5A filed down
the corridor to the canteen. "You're
acting really weird."

"I've already told you," said Maddy

coolly. "It's not *my* fault you don't believe me. Even though I've never, ever lied to you, not ever." Rachel rolled her eyes, and didn't answer.

As the class neared the canteen, Maddy saw Sherry jostle Jessica Simmons, a new girl in their class. She'd been taunting Jessica ever since she first arrived.

"Hey, thanks for loaning us your DS, Jess," sneered Sherry. Jo and Jo sniggered, and Jessica's face reddened. She was even shorter than Maddy, with long pale hair and skinny legs like pipe cleaners.

"I, um – I need it back," she mumbled. "It was a present from my mum – she'll be asking me where it is—"

"*Ooh*, a present from her *mum-my*!" crooned Sherry, flipping back her

76

dark blonde hair. "Well, don't worry, Jessie-Wessie – we'll give it back later. Maybe!" She and her friends laughed as they headed into the canteen.

Maddy's fists clenched at the defeated look on Jessica's face. Oh, how she longed to give Sherry a good telling-off – if only she had the courage!

"*Ouch!*" she burst out suddenly. A sharp claw had dug into her side. And the weight in her pocket felt different – heavier, warmer. Greykin! Maddy grabbed Rachel's arm and pulled her into the girls' loos.

"What are you doing?" cried Rachel.

Making sure that they were alone, Maddy dragged her friend into one of

77

the cubicles, crowding in after her and closing the door.

"*Mad*-dy . . ."

She reached into her pocket. Flattening her palm so that Greykin could climb onto it, Maddy held him up in front of Rachel. Her best friend gaped wordlessly at the tiny cat, the blood abruptly leaving her face.

"Greykin, this is Rachel." Maddy grinned. "She's very, very sorry that she didn't believe me – aren't you, Rache?"

Rachel's mouth closed with a snap. "Maddy!" she whispered, clutching Maddy's arm. "It's – it's real!"

Greykin yawned, showing a mouthful of tiny pointed teeth. "That's a very tiresome reaction," he complained. "Whatever happened to

78

'Pleased to meet you'?"

Rachel goggled at the sound of
his voice. For a moment Maddy
thought she might pass out. "I'm . . .
sorry," she murmured finally. "I – um
– pleased to meet you."

"Yes, charmed," said Greykin
briskly, lashing his tail from side to
side on Maddy's palm. "But we've

more serious matters to discuss, I'm afraid."

Maddy caught her breath. "Have your whiskers tingled?"

Greykin nodded. "It's that girl – the one who took the toy from the other child. She's the problem. She must be stopped from tormenting her."

Maddy's stomach did a somersault. "*Sherry?*" she gasped. "But—"

"What are you talking about?" put in Rachel, her eyes wide behind her glasses.

Maddy quickly explained, and Rachel stared at her in horror. "*You*, stop Sherry? But – but how?"

"There are ways," said Greykin firmly. His golden gaze glinted up at them. "Trust me."

81

That afternoon Rachel got permission to go home with Maddy. Once safe in Maddy's bedroom, the two girls sat cross-legged on the carpet, sharing a plate of chocolate biscuits as Greykin prowled between them.

"Would you like some, Greykin?" asked Rachel eagerly, holding out a crumb.

He sniffed at it, and his furry face winced. "No, thank you," he said with barely concealed disgust. "It's *sweet*."

His expression changed when Maddy burrowed in her school bag and brought out a leftover bit of lunch-time sandwich.

"That's more like it!" he said. She put a sliver of ham beside

the biscuits, and
he bounded onto
the plate and ate
it daintily, purring
his approval.

"What are
we going to do about Sherry,
though?" asked Maddy as he finished.
She pulled her knees up to her chest.
"Greykin, you don't understand what
she's like. *I* can't stop her – she'd kill
me! And you . . . well, you're only
five centimetres tall."

"Size isn't everything," said
Greykin, looking affronted. "I
suppose you'd rather I was a big
galumphing dog."

"No, of *course* not," soothed
Maddy quickly. She ran her finger
down his velvety grey back. "I

wouldn't trade you for anything. Not
even for – for a whole roomful of
diamonds!"

Greykin beamed. "Well, it *is* true
that a king's ransom was once offered
for the three of us," he said modestly.
"Many centuries ago, but one doesn't
forget. Now, then!" he went on as
Maddy and Rachel gaped at each
other. "The first thing we must do
is examine our information. Tell me
everything you know about Sherry."

Collecting herself, Maddy tried to
think. "Well, she's really horrid, and
everyone hates her. And she's tall."

"And *big*," added Rachel with
a shudder. "And she's always
scowling—"

"Yes, and she has a really loud
voice, and—" Maddy broke off.

Paw Power

Greykin was shaking his tiny head.

"Not what she *looks* like," he said gently. "What do you know about her? Home situation, age, siblings?"

Maddy and Rachel exchanged uncertain glances. Suddenly Maddy realized that she hardly knew anything at all about Sherry's life.

"Well . . . I suppose she's nine, like us," she said finally.

Rachel nodded. "And she doesn't have any brothers or sisters at our school, but she might have some that aren't. And, um . . ." Her face screwed up in thought. "That's all I know."

"Me too," said Maddy. "Oh, hang on – she's got these two awful friends, Jo Perkins and Jo Pearson. They back her up in *everything*."

Greykin fell silent, twitching the tip of his tail. "It's not very much information, is it?"

Maddy's cheeks reddened. "Not really," she admitted. "But we're not exactly friends with her."

"No, we try to *avoid* her," said Rachel. "Everyone does!"

"Nevertheless, we must find a way to stop this girl." Greykin stepped off the plate and leaped onto Maddy's leg, settling down on her thigh. Rachel looked on longingly, and Maddy felt a shiver of pride. Oh, she was so lucky!

"As I see it, there are three options," said Greykin, curling his paws under his chunky body. "One: we separate Jessica from Sherry."

"But they go to school together," protested Rachel.

"Option two: we persuade Sherry to

leave Jessica alone."

The two girls burst out laughing. "You mean we should just *ask* her, and maybe she'll stop?" cried Maddy. "Oh, right!"

Greykin smiled. "You'd be surprised what the powers of persuasion can do. But let's think about option three. Tell me everything you know about Jessica, both of you."

Maddy thought hard. "Well, she just started at our school this term. She's shorter than me, and she seems very quiet and shy . . . um . . ."

"Didn't someone say she has a pony she rides at weekends?" said Rachel, adjusting her glasses.

"Oh, yes!" recalled Maddy. "That was Sandra; she has a pony at the same stables."

Paw Power

"So she's not utterly without courage, then," mused Greykin, narrowing his eyes in thought. "Perhaps we just need to help it along a bit."

Maddy pictured Jessica's scared-rabbit face. "I don't think she's all *that* brave," she said doubtfully. In fact, Jessica reminded her of how *she* felt sometimes.

Greykin chuckled. "In which case, Sherry will be doubly startled when her victim suddenly stands up to her."

"*What?*" gasped Maddy.

Chapter Four

"There's no *way* we could get Jessica to do that!" cried Rachel at the same time.

Standing up on Maddy's thigh, the little cat pulled himself into a long, luxurious stretch. "We have more resources than you think," he said, settling back onto his haunches. "Now, listen. What am I doing?"

A deep rumble started in his throat, increasing in volume until it reverberated through the room.

"You're purring," said Maddy blankly.

"Exactly! And why do cats purr?"

Maddy and Rachel looked at each other. Was this a trick question? "Um . . . because they're happy?" ventured Rachel.

"Only sometimes," Greykin

corrected her. "We also purr when
we're distressed, to calm ourselves
down."

"Oh, I didn't know that," said
Maddy, interested despite herself.
"But, Greykin, how—"

"And *my* purr can do even more
than that," Greykin informed them
proudly. "Maddy, you just need to
keep me in your pocket and stay close
to Jessica so that she can hear my Purr
without realizing it. It will give her

strength she didn't know she had."

"Will it, like – *hypnotize* her?" gasped Rachel, rising up onto her knees.

Greykin grimaced. "It's a far subtler process, but I suppose you could make that comparison. Maddy, all you'll have to do then is suggest to Jessica that she should stand up for herself, and that will be that!"

"*Really?*" breathed Maddy.

Glancing at each other, she and Rachel began to smile.

"Can you imagine it?" giggled Rachel.

Maddy nodded, barely able to get the words out. "Sherry – Sherry will be like *this*!" She made a dumbfounded, slack-jawed face.

"No, *this*," cried Rachel, making

her eyes bulge out as if she'd seen a zombie.

Suddenly the two girls were howling with laughter. Greykin leaped clear as Maddy drummed her heels on the carpet. "Really," he said mildly. "You'd think you two had never experienced a bit of magic before!"

Finally they calmed down enough to decide on a plan. "I think you should do it on Friday," said Rachel eagerly. "'Cos then we break for half-term, so it'll be like a treat for everyone before the holiday!"

Greykin chuckled, swishing his tail from side to side. "Apart from Sherry, of course."

"Perfect!" said Maddy.

Secretly, she had another reason

93

for wanting to wait a few days: once Sherry's bullying had been stopped, Greykin would become a ceramic cat again. Her throat tightened, and she pushed the thought away. She had Greykin *now* – that was all that mattered.

With their plan now neatly in place, the two girls spent the rest of the afternoon playing with Greykin. Rachel was entranced by the tiny cat's jewellery-box bed.

"Why don't we build a ladder for him?" she suggested. "That way he can climb up and down the chest of drawers on his own."

"Ooh, yes!" exclaimed Maddy. She found a long strip of firm cardboard, and they made steps with bits of Blu-Tack. Soon Greykin was

95

prowling up and down it, purring his approval.

Rachel watched him closely, hungry with curiosity. Maddy grinned. Her friend was very scientific, and Maddy knew she must be dying to find out all she could about the cats!

"So, Greykin," said Rachel, casually polishing her glasses on her jumper. "Where do you and the other two cats come from?"

"Didn't Maddy tell you?" Greykin leaped off the ladder onto the carpet. "She found us at an antique fair."

Rachel frowned. "No, I mean—"

"Can't catch me!" cried Greykin suddenly, jumping over her foot. He darted about the room like a furry pinball, and the two girls were soon shrieking with laughter as they lunged after him. After several minutes they slumped to the floor, panting and giggling.

Greykin sat perched atop one of Maddy's pink rabbit bedroom slippers. "Lovely!" he exclaimed, swishing his tail. "It's been decades since I've had a good romp."

Rachel straightened, her blue eyes instantly alert. "So . . . how old *are* you, then?"

Greykin began washing himself,

running his paw over his face. "I'm so sorry," he said pleasantly. "I'm a bit deaf in one ear. You'll have to speak more clearly."

"*How old*—" began Rachel.

"No, I still can't make it out," interrupted Greykin. "Perhaps you could take elocution lessons."

Maddy bit her lip to keep from laughing. She was curious about the cats too, of course, but Rachel looked as if she were about to explode!

The bedroom door opened, and Maddy's mum stuck her head in. "*What* have you two been doing up here? It sounded like stampeding elephants!"

"Just a game," said Maddy hastily. Out of the corner of her eye she could see that Greykin had become ceramic again, freezing in place beside one of the rabbit's pink ears.

Her mother shook her head. "Rachel, your mum's here."

Rachel tore her gaze away from

Greykin. "Oh! I – I didn't hear the doorbell."

Maddy's mother laughed. "I'm not surprised! We're just having a cup of tea, but don't be long, all right?"

After she had left, Rachel gathered up her things. "He's not going to tell me anything, is he?" she said glumly.

"I guess he wants to keep his past a secret," said Maddy. "But it doesn't really matter, does it? The important thing is that he's *real*."

Paw Power

Rachel gazed at the other two cats on Maddy's desk. "I suppose you're right," she sighed finally. "But, oh, Maddy . . . I'd give *anything* to know more about them!"

Chapter Five

"Get off those swings, it's our turn," Sherry was bellowing at a pair of Year Threes as Maddy entered the school playground on Friday morning. They scurried away, and Sherry sat down smugly.

"Come on, let's have a contest," she said to the two Jos. "I bet I win. I *always* win!"

Maddy stopped short. She'd had so much fun with Greykin these last few

Paw Power

days that she hadn't really thought about what was coming, but now all at once her stomach felt cold.

Rachel appeared beside her. "Have you got him?" she asked, her eyes shining.

Maddy nodded. "In my pocket – he's still ceramic. But listen, Rache, what if – what if it goes wrong somehow?"

Glancing across the playground,
she saw Jessica standing huddled in
her jacket, on her own as usual – no
one in 5A dared to make friends with
her, because of Sherry. Maddy felt
an anxious pang. *How* could Jessica
ever stand up to Sherry, even with
magic?

"It won't go wrong," said Rachel,
squeezing her arm. "It'll be *brilliant*.
Remember?" She made the wide-eyed
zombie face again, staggering about
the playground.

Paw Power

Maddy burst out giggling despite herself. Rachel was right. Greykin was so old and wise – he *must* know what he was doing!

As the day went on she became more and more excited, peering at Sherry from under her long hair. Oh, she had such a surprise in store! Maddy watched the clock impatiently, waiting for lunch time.

Finally the bell rang, and 5A trooped to the canteen. "I'll sit somewhere else," whispered Rachel. "It would be too suspicious, both of us suddenly being nice to Jessica at once!"

"What?" said Maddy in alarm. She'd assumed Rachel would be with her. "But what if Sherry—"

"Go *on.*" Rachel gave her a shove.

Taking a deep breath, Maddy
headed over to the table where Jessica
always sat alone. "Can – can I sit
here?" she asked.

Jessica looked up, startled, as
Maddy put her packed lunch next
to Jessica's school one. "Oh! Well,
sure." She scraped her chair over to
make room, gaping at Maddy.

"So . . . where are you from?"
Maddy felt the small, solid weight
of Greykin as he came to life in her
pocket. Sherry hadn't noticed her yet,
she saw with relief. She was still in
the lunch queue, shoving the boy in
front of her and talking loudly.

Jessica's face lit up. "Bristol."

Purrr. Purrrrrrr. Purrrrrrrrrrrrrr.

Maddy started. It felt like there
was an engine in her pocket. "Oh!

Um – did you like it there?"

"It was OK." A look of dread crossed Jessica's face. Twisting in her seat, Maddy saw Sherry nudging the spiky-haired Jo and pointing at them. *No!*

Chapter Five

The Purr continued, louder than before. Maddy found it amazing that the whole canteen didn't hear it, but not even *Jessica* seemed to. Maddy tried to angle herself so that Greykin was pointing right at her.

"Tell me more about Bristol," she said. "It's – it's got a harbour, right?"

Jessica's gaze flicked nervously behind Maddy. "Sherry's watching us," she whispered.

"I know," Maddy whispered back. "Just ignore her."

Jessica's jaw dropped. "*Ignore* her?"

"Sure," said Maddy desperately. "I'm not scared of her; why should you be? She's just a big, cowardly bully."

Paw Power

Jessica gazed at Maddy as if she were the bravest person on the planet. She scraped her chair a bit closer to Maddy's.

Maddy saw Sherry and the two Jos starting forward, weaving through the tables. Oh, Greykin, *hurry*! "Why did you move here?" she managed.

Purrr, PURRRRRRR!

Suddenly Jessica sat bolt upright, her eyes wide. Maddy held her breath as a faint hint of colour came into the other girl's cheeks and she shook her head as if to clear it.

"Jessica?" Maddy leaned forward.

Jessica's thin shoulders straightened. She gave Maddy a

considering look. "So . . . you're really not afraid of Sherry, then?"

"No, and you shouldn't be either!" Maddy glanced over her shoulder, her heart thudding.

"You're right!" Jessica stood up so abruptly that she knocked her chair over. Maddy watched, open-mouthed, as she strode up to the larger girl.

"Listen, Sherry!" she said, hands on hips. "I've had just about enough of you!"

Sherry goggled down at her. "Er . . ."

"You've been picking on me ever since I got here, and you can just stop it right now," said Jessica. She took another step forward. Sherry actually backed away, looking startled.

Maddy stifled a wild giggle.

110

Chapter Five

Jessica's chin was thrust out, her eyes narrowed firmly. The dining room fell silent as the children stared at the scene in wonder. A few tables away, Rachel sat dreamy-eyed, as if she were watching the most wonderful film ever.

Sherry recovered herself with an attempt at a sneer. "Yeah, well . . . how are you going to make me?"

"Don't push me, Sherry," said Jessica in a low voice.

Sherry gulped, and glanced desperately at the two Jos. They seemed as stunned as she was.

"I'm not scared of *you*," Jessica went on disdainfully. "Neither is Maddy."

"*Maddy?*" Sherry's tone sharpened. She looked across the canteen.

112

Paw Power

Maddy quickly busied herself with unwrapping her sandwich.

"No, we're not scared of you at all," said Jessica, tossing her blonde hair. "Why should we be? That's what Maddy says. She says you're just a big, cowardly bully!"

"Oh, she does, does she?" snarled Sherry.

"Sit down, girls," called one of the teachers.

"Yeah, so *back off*," said Jessica. And with a final hard look at Sherry, she turned on her heel and sauntered away.

She sat down next to Maddy again – and blinked. All at once her face lost its confident expression, turning pale and scared-rabbit again. "I – I stood up to Sherry!" she gasped, her hand flying to her mouth. "Oh my gosh, I can't believe I *did* that! How—"

"Yeah, great." Maddy's voice came out in a squeak. "Well, um – nice talking to you, Jessica. Got to go now!" She grabbed up her lunch and scurried over to Rachel's table. Her best friend was biting her thumbnail.

"Wow," she said weakly as Maddy

114

sat down beside her. "The Purr really works, doesn't it?"

"What am I going to do?" cried Maddy. "Sherry's going to *kill* me!"

Rachel's mouth twisted. "Um . . . maybe it's not *that* bad. I mean, Sherry's never noticed you before, has she? So why would she bother now?"

"Do you think?" said Maddy, hardly daring to hope.

Rachel nodded quickly. "Of course! Well . . . maybe."

The two girls stared at each other. As one, they peeked over their shoulders. Sherry and her gang were sitting huddled at a nearby table, whispering and shooting venomous looks in Maddy's direction.

Suddenly Maddy had a very, very bad feeling.

Chapter Six

"It's unfortunate," admitted Greykin later that afternoon.

He was prowling about on Maddy's maths worksheet as she sat fretting at her desk. She had started on her homework to try and take her mind off things, but she'd never felt less able to concentrate in her life.

"*Unfortunate?*" she burst out. "Greykin, did you see her face? I mean, no, of course you didn't, but—"

Chapter Six

"Worse than that, I'm afraid,"
said Greykin. He paused at problem
twelve, peering down at it with a furry
frown. "This should be thirty-seven,
not thirty-five."

"What do you mean, *worse than
that*?" asked Maddy. Her hands felt
clammy as she made the correction.

She and the tiny cat were alone.
Rachel had wanted desperately to

come home with Maddy again, but she and her family were leaving for Cornwall the next morning, and her mum had said they had too much to do. In a strange way, Maddy was glad. It was lovely to have Greykin all to herself – even at such a time as this.

Greykin sighed and sat down, his tail curling about the number seven. "Well – we cats have rather superior hearing, you know. Sherry and her cohorts were plotting what to do to you after half-term. I'm afraid their plan is for you to become their next victim."

Chapter Six

Maddy's heart seemed to shrivel in her chest as she stared at him. "Me? But – oh, Greykin! What *now*?"

She jumped as her door opened.

"Thought you might like a treat," said her mother cheerfully, coming into the room. "How are you getting on?"

"Oh . . . fine," said Maddy as her mother put a small plate of biscuits on the desk. Greykin had instantly become ceramic again, his painted eyes vacant. "Thanks, Mum."

"Oh look, it's your little cat! Is he keeping you company?" Maddy's mother laughed as she picked up Greykin, turning him over in her hands.

Maddy nodded, wishing fervently that she would put Greykin down and

120

leave. Then her cheeks reddened. Her mum was holding Greykin upside-down, peering at his bum!

"Mum, *don't*!" She grabbed Greykin away.

Chapter Six

Her mother blinked. "Don't what? I was just noticing that he doesn't have one of those little holes on his underside. See?" Taking the tiny cat back, she turned him over again, pointing. "I thought all ceramic figurines did . . . it's a bit strange. I wonder if these two do?"

Maddy gulped as Mum reached for the other cats. What if she thought it was so strange that she decided to take the set away, and study them in more detail?

"Mum, I'm busy," she said.

"Hmm?" Her mother frowned as she inspected the black cat's stomach.

"*Mum*," insisted Maddy, her heart thudding.

Maddy's mother shook her head and placed the black cat back on the desk.

Paw Power

"Odd . . . All right, love, enjoy the biscuits. I've some studying of my own to do."

Maddy sagged in relief as she left the room. Greykin rippled back into life and regarded her coolly, flicking his ears.

"Don't look at me like that! I couldn't stop her," said Maddy. She adjusted the black cat so that he was entwined with the long-haired tabby once more.

"To think that *I*, who have been fêted by royalty . . ." Greykin shook his head with a weary sigh. "I suppose it's only to be expected in this uncouth age. Not like the glory days of Persia."

"Persia?" echoed Maddy. "Is that where you—"

"In any event, leaving my indignity aside, there's a problem that needs discussing," broke in Greykin. He began to groom himself, attacking his thick grey fur with long strokes of his tongue.

Sherry. A shiver ran through Maddy as she imagined returning to school, with Sherry and her gang waiting in the playground like vultures. Then she relaxed as the answer came to her.

"But, Greykin, it's easy! All you have to do is use the Purr on *me*, right? Then I'll be able to stand up to Sherry too!"

Greykin stopped grooming and cocked his round head to one side. "Perhaps," he said thoughtfully. "Shall we test it? Close your eyes, and imagine meeting Sherry in the schoolyard. If you touch my fur, it will make it more vivid for you," he added.

Hesitantly, Maddy rested a finger on Greykin's velvety fur. Closing her eyes, she pictured herself in the playground again.

She could see it very clearly. She was standing by the slide wearing her blue jacket, and she could feel the cold air, hear the squeak of the swings – and see Sherry Newton and the two Jos advancing towards her, smiling unpleasantly.

Maddy took a deep breath. *Be brave, be brave*, she thought. Where was the Purr? And then all at once she heard it, a deep rumbling like the ocean's roar.

Purr, PURRRR, PURRRRRR!

Maddy straightened as courage pulsed through her, tingling from her head down to her toes. Oh, what a lovely feeling! Sherry and the two Jos were almost on her now. Sherry's face was alight with glee.

Paw Power

"I'm not afraid of *you*," Maddy started to say scornfully . . . and then stopped in confusion. A tiny voice inside her was whispering, *But I am, really. It's just the Purr that's making me brave; it's not me at all.*

And with that Maddy could feel the courage leaving her, swirling away like water down a drain. The Purr grew fainter, until she could hardly hear it at all . . . and then it was gone.

Sherry's eyes glinted as she loomed over Maddy with an evil grin. Heart pounding, Maddy tore her finger away from Greykin's back before she could imagine what happened next.

The playground scene vanished. She was still safe in her room, sitting at her desk. The little cat was perched on her maths paper, watching her keenly.

"Oh, Greykin, it didn't work!" wailed Maddy. "I mean, it – it sort of started to, but then . . ." She trailed off in dismay.

Paw Power

Greykin nodded sympathetically. "Yes, I was afraid that might happen. You see, the Purr doesn't always work when one knows about it – particularly if the fear is too great."

"Oh," said Maddy in a small voice. She must be a bigger coward than she'd thought if Greykin's Purr couldn't even help her out in her imagination!

Greykin padded across the desk and rubbed his head comfortingly against her thumb. "Don't worry, Maddy. The Purr is only minor magic – it can't solve everything. What we need now is

some real paw power! And fortunately
we have much stronger weapons than
the Purr in our arsenal."

Maddy wasn't sure what an arsenal
was, but Greykin's meaning was clear
enough. "We do?"

"We do." Greykin nosed Maddy's
hand, and she turned it over so that he
could step onto her palm. She raised
him up to face-level, and he beamed
at her.

"Maddy . . . how would you like
to have magical powers of your own?"

"Now, the first thing is to just relax,"
instructed Greykin. "Try flexing your
knees a bit."

Standing in the meadow at the
bottom of their back garden, Maddy
bobbed up and down. She glanced

over her shoulder at the house,
praying that Jack wouldn't suddenly
appear.

"You're not concentrating," said
Greykin. He was perched on her
shoulder like a small grey parrot.
"You need to get into the right
mindset. Think *cat*."

"Cat," murmured Maddy, dipping
up and down. "Cat, cat, cat."

131

Chapter Six

What would it be like, she
wondered nervously, to suddenly have
a cat's physical prowess? For that,
incredibly, was what Greykin had told
her would happen. Each of the tiny
cats had the ability to give Maddy
powers of her own – and Greykin's
magic would allow her to perform
amazing feline feats.

She stopped bobbing and cleared
her throat. "Er . . . it's not going to
hurt, is it?"

"*Hurt?* To take on a cat's grace and
strength?" Greykin sounded insulted.
"Now then, are you ready?"

"I suppose." Maddy wiped her
palms on her jeans.

Greykin sat very still on her
shoulder. After a moment he began
to speak again – an odd mix of

foreign words and a cat's meows and chirrups. There was silence as he finished.

Maddy began to fidget. She felt exactly the same as before. "Greykin, I don't think it— *Oh!*"

She yelped as a rush of tingly power crackled through her. It felt as if her hair were standing on end!

"Try a leap," cried Greykin, digging his tiny claws into her jumper.

Maddy noticed that her knees felt different: springier, and more powerful. She crouched down – and leaped.

All at once she was more than two metres up, hurtling through the air like a rocket. "Aargh!" she shrieked, her legs wheeling. There was a dizzying blur of trees, clouds, the ground – and then she landed with a *thump*.

Paw Power

"*Ow.*" Maddy sat up, rubbing her arm.

Greykin had jumped clear when she landed, and was now sitting on a nearby tree stump. "Are you all right?" he asked, his furry face creased in concern.

"You said it wouldn't hurt!" accused Maddy.

"I didn't *precisely* say that," corrected Greykin gently. "There can sometimes be teething problems."

Maddy thought he really might have mentioned this before. She struggled to her feet and brushed herself down.

Bounding through the grass towards Maddy's foot, Greykin scampered up her jeans and top. "You mustn't be discouraged. You just need to let go, and trust your new cat instincts! Try

135

leaping with your
eyes closed."

Maddy gaped at
him. "But – I'll crash
into something!"

"Unlikely," said
Greykin, swishing
his tail. "The field's
empty. Try it and
see."

Somehow Maddy found herself
bending at the knees again, her eyes
screwed tightly shut. She took a deep
breath . . . and leaped.

Without the view of the ground
below, the whiz of air rushing past
didn't seem nearly so alarming.
Maddy's legs seemed to know
what to do on their own this time,
and flexed gracefully beneath her

136

as she landed.

"Oh!" she gasped, whirling about. She was standing upright, three metres away from where she'd started.

Greykin purred into her ear. "You see? One hates to say I told you so, but—"

"I did it!" Maddy gave an excited pirouette, her long brown hair fanning out. "Greykin, I really did it!"

Soon she was leaping all over the field – landing, crouching, springing. Her heart sang with excitement. What luck that there were so few houses close by!

"Well done," said Greykin finally. "I

think we can move on to climbing."

Maddy's high spirits vanished as she stood at the base of the oak tree that rose from a corner of the meadow. It had to be at least fifteen metres tall! The tree's branches seemed to spin dizzily as she stared upwards.

"Um, Greykin . . . I don't really like heights very much," admitted Maddy. "They – they make me feel really odd, like my

stomach's whirling around and I can't
breathe—"

"That won't bother you now,"
promised Greykin. "Cats love heights
– the higher, the better!" His golden
eyes gleamed. "Just look up, say to
yourself, *That's where I'm going*
– and go!"

Maddy swallowed. She placed her
hands on the oak's rough surface and
gazed up at the tiny branches near
the top. "That's – that's where I'm
going," she faltered.

Whoosh! Suddenly she
was scampering up the
tree like a monkey. A
starling squawked in
alarm, darting out of her
way. Leaves and branches
raced past, until suddenly

Maddy was perched high up in the oak.

"Wheee!" she cried, clinging to its swaying branches. "Greykin, look! We can see for miles!"

A patchwork of fields and houses was laid out below her, like the view from an aeroplane. Maddy stared curiously at her own house. How funny to look down on its grey slate roof!

As she watched, a male figure appeared at one of the first-floor windows. Dad! Maddy giggled. He looked even smaller than her Barbie doll.

Her giggle died abruptly as she realized that her father could see her too.

The window slid open. "*Maddy!*"

140

he bellowed. "What on *earth* are you doing up there?"

"Nothing," Maddy called weakly back. Jack and Mum appeared behind him, gaping up at her. "Just . . . climbing."

"Get down at once!" shouted her dad. "No, wait – I'm coming out! Don't move!"

Unfortunately, climbing back down the tree turned out to be a great deal harder than climbing up. As her family stood on the ground gawping, Maddy slipped and slithered her way down.

"Careful!" yelled Maddy's mum. "Oh, Ted, be ready to catch her if she falls."

Hidden by her long hair, Greykin clung to Maddy's shoulder, whispering encouragement. "That's

it . . . there's a branch just
by your left foot . . ."

"Why isn't the power
working *now*?" hissed
Maddy. She pawed
the air with her foot,
and heard her mother
gasp.

"Ah . . . well, it is,"
admitted Greykin,
peering downwards.
"I'm afraid we're
not quite so nimble
climbing down trees
as we are going up
them."

Finally Maddy
dropped the last
couple of metres to
the ground. Greykin

had crawled under her collar, safely out of sight. She wished glumly that she could do the same, somehow.

Her mother scooped her into a tight hug, and then held her at arm's  length. "Don't *ever* do that again!" she exclaimed. "My gosh, you nearly gave me a heart attack."

Maddy's father was stroking his beard, looking bemused. "I thought you were afraid of heights," he pointed out.

"I . . . just thought it might be fun," said Maddy. Her cheeks felt on fire. "I'm sorry. I won't do it again."

Guiltily she crossed her fingers behind her back. But it wasn't *too*

144

awful a lie, she comforted herself.
Her parents didn't know that she was
protected by cat magic.

"Wow, you were right at the very
top!" Jack bounced on his toes. "Will
you teach *me* to do that? Please,
Maddy? Please?"

"*No!*" said their parents in unison.
"Don't even think of it," added Mum
with a shiver. "Now come on – back
inside!"

Maddy couldn't sleep that night. The
wonder of being chosen by the three
cats bubbled through her, stronger
than ever before. She was just *herself*,
Maddy Lloyd – yet this amazing thing
had happened to her!

She crept out of bed and peered
into her jewellery box. Greykin lay

145

curled up on his rainbow cushion of
scrunchies, his tiny sides rising and
falling.

"Greykin?" she murmured. She
touched him gently with her index
finger.

"Mm?" he said drowsily, opening a
single golden eye.

Maddy glanced at her desk. She
could see the black cat and the tabby
shining in the moonlight. "I was just

curious about the other cats," she whispered. "What are they like?"

The little cat stretched. "I shall refrain from quoting a rather tiresome maxim about curiosity and cats," he said with a yawn. "The three of us are each quite unique – though of course we all have a cat's grace and charm."

"Yes, but what are the other two *like*?" pressed Maddy.

Greykin's eyes squinted in a feline smile. "You'll find out when it's their turn to meet you. May I go back to sleep now?"

"Just one more thing," whispered Maddy eagerly. "You said that the magic powers the other two cats can give me are different from yours – what are they?"

Greykin curled himself back into a

ball, tucking his nose under his tail. When his voice came again, it was muffled. "Let's just say I don't think you'll be disappointed when the time comes."

That week Maddy practised her new skills whenever she could, which wasn't easy with Jack hanging about. But whenever he went to play with a friend, or was busy with something

inside, Maddy leaped and climbed to her heart's content – though she kept a careful eye on the house.

On Friday afternoon, after a particularly energetic session, Greykin's ears twitched as if he were listening to something. "That's enough for now," he said from his place on her hand.

Maddy gazed at him in disappointment. "But I could go on

for loads longer!"

Greykin shook his head. "Yes, but—"
He stopped abruptly, freezing in place
as he became ceramic.

"Who are you talking to?" said a
voice.

Maddy whirled round. "What
are *you* doing here?" she snapped,
tucking Greykin quickly in her
pocket.

Jack shrugged. He was
hanging onto the wooden
gate that led into the
meadow, finishing
off a choc ice. "Why
are you spending so
much time down
here now? I bet
you're up to something!"
Maddy clenched her fists.

Paw Power

How was she supposed to practise with Jack around? Suddenly a wonderful idea came to her. Would it work, with Greykin in his ceramic form? She didn't know, but it was definitely worth a try!

She smiled sweetly at her little brother. "You're right," she said. "But it's a secret."

"I can keep a secret!" burst out Jack, scrambling off the gate and sprinting over to her.

"Well . . ." Maddy put on a doubtful look.

"Please!" begged Jack, tugging at her sleeve. "Please tell me, Maddy, please, please, *pur-leeease.*"

"All right," she decided. "But you can't tell anybody. Here's the secret – I've found out how to jump *really,*

151

really high! Do you want me to show you?"

Jack nodded vehemently.

"First, you sit like this." Maddy sank onto her haunches in the grass. Jack squatted beside her, his eyes wide.

"Then you do some little baby hops." Maddy hopped up and down in place, holding back a giggle as Jack did the same. "Then, you say . . . *Ooga booga booga!*"

Jack stopped hopping. "Ooga *what?*"

"*Ooga booga booga,*" said Maddy. "Like this!" Closing her eyes, she chanted, "*Ooga booga booga! Ooga booga booga!*" *Cat*, she thought to herself. *Cat . . .*

The tingling sensation rushed through her, like cool water on a

Paw Power

sizzling-hot day. *Whoosh!* All at once
Maddy sprang nearly two metres
into the air, narrowly missing Jack's
head.

"*Wow!*" he burst out as she landed.
He leaped up, punching the air.

"Maddy, that was *great!*"

Maddy nodded modestly. "But you
have to practise *loads* before you can

do it. And it has to be in secret," she added. "So you can't hang around me all the time, or it won't work."

"I won't!" gasped Jack. He squatted down again, closing his eyes. "*Ooga booga booga*," he muttered. "*Ooga booga booga*."

Maddy strolled back to the house, feeling very pleased with herself. That should take care of Jack for a while! And best of all, if he *did* tell anyone, they'd never believe him.

When Maddy got back inside, her mother was just hanging up the phone.

"That was Rachel's mum," she said. "They're back from Cornwall, but she says all Rachel did was mope about, missing you. Do you fancy having her round to stay the night tonight?"

Paw Power

"Yes!" squealed Maddy, jumping up and down. Oh, how perfect. She could hardly wait to show Rachel her new powers!

But when Rachel arrived later that afternoon, there was a group of older boys playing football in the meadow. The two girls went up to Maddy's room, where she quickly filled her best friend in on what she had been doing over the break.

Rachel gazed at the ceramic cat in wonder as he sat between them on the duvet. "Oh, Mad, I can't wait to see! But I wish Greykin would come to life," she added wistfully, touching his smooth back. "The whole time I was away, I kept thinking I must have dreamed it all."

But Greykin didn't wake up again until after dinner. And when he did, he wasn't pleased.

"The powers are *not* to be used to play frivolous tricks on your little brother," he scolded Maddy. He was sitting on her bedside table beside her ballerina lamp, as

though the ballerina had a pet panther.
"As I started to tell you earlier, the
other two cats were tired out!"

Rachel watched Greykin with
shining eyes. "Oh, you really *are*
real!" she whispered.

The cat gave her a withering look.
He turned back to Maddy, lashing his
tail from side to side. "The other two
have only so much *ka* at any given

time – you're not to waste it."

"I'm sorry," said Maddy. Sitting on
the bed, she glanced guiltily at the
small black cat and the tabby with the
white-masked face. "I didn't mean . . ."

Greykin sighed. Leaping across to
her, he nuzzled her hand. "I know
you didn't. But they already have to
provide the magic for *me* to come to
life. When you use your cat powers,
they have to work even harder. So you
must always stop when I tell you to,
or else your powers might vanish until
they've had a chance to rest."

"All right," agreed Maddy, relieved
that he didn't seem cross any more.

"Greykin, look – I've got something
for you!" said Rachel eagerly.

She drew out some tiny scraps of
hamburger she'd saved from dinner.

Greykin purred his approval. As he ate, Rachel hugged herself with delight. "Oh, Maddy, I can still hardly believe it. There really *is* magic!"

Later, the mood became more sombre. Maddy told Rachel what Greykin had overheard – that *she* was due to be Sherry's next victim once they got back to school.

The two girls were in their

nightclothes by then, perched on
Maddy's bed. "Oh, no!" breathed
Rachel. "Maddy, what are you going
to do?"

"I should have thought it was
obvious," commented Greykin, curled
up warmly on Maddy's knee.

Maddy frowned. Though she'd
been practising her new cat powers
whenever she could, she suddenly
realized that she wasn't the least bit
certain how she was supposed to use
them against Sherry.

"Er . . ." She and Rachel glanced at
each other. Maddy cleared her throat.
"Actually . . . could you tell us?"

The little cat stretched out his front
paws, yawning. "It's simple. You just
need to use your superior strength to
force Sherry into submission."

Paw Power

Maddy's mouth dropped open. "You mean . . . you want me to *fight* her? But, Greykin, I can't do that!"

His golden eyes blinked up at her. "Why ever not?"

"Because – because she'd get into all sorts of trouble, that's why!" spluttered Rachel. "Besides, it's

wrong to fight."

Greykin flexed his tiny claws. "It's
how we cats solve things. And I must
say, I've always had the impression
that it was rather a human trait, as
well."

"Maybe it is – but that doesn't mean
it *should* be," said Maddy firmly.
"We've got to think of something
else, Greykin."

"Hang on – *I* know!" Rachel
bounced up on her knees. Her
glasses slid down her nose, and
she straightened them impatiently.
"Maddy, what's Sherry's favourite
thing in the world?"

Maddy lifted a shoulder. "Being
horrible?"

"Besides that!" Rachel's face was lit
with excitement. "She loves *winning*,

doesn't she? No matter what she's doing, she always has to win!"

Greykin nodded slowly from Maddy's knee. "Ah, I see. Yes, it has definite possibilities."

Maddy stared at them in confusion. "What does?"

"Don't you get it?" Rachel clutched Maddy's arm. "What if you challenged Sherry to a contest, in front of everybody? Like, running or jumping or something?"

Maddy caught her breath as she suddenly saw what Rachel was driving at. "Oh! And then I'd beat her—"

"By a considerable margin," chuckled Greykin.

"She'd be completely humiliated!" finished Rachel, throwing her arms

out triumphantly. "Oh, Maddy, she'd back right off then, I know she would. Problem solved!"

The three of them sat up for hours, planning. When they finally went to bed, Maddy lay awake for a long time, smiling up at the ceiling. She'd never have believed it last Friday, but she was actually looking forward to going back to school. Beating Sherry would be the most amazing thing in the world!

Chapter Seven

When Maddy arrived at school on the first day after half-term, she saw Jessica standing in the centre of the playground, with an excited group from Maddy's class clustered around her.

"Jessica, tell us about how you stood up to Sherry!" pleaded a girl called Beth.

"Yeah, it was *brilliant*," said someone else. "How did you ever dare?"

Edging through the crowd, Maddy
thought that Jessica looked a bit
panicked by all the attention. "I
– um – I don't really remember," she
mumbled, her cheeks reddening as
she hunched into her jacket. "It just
sort of came over me . . ."

She spotted Maddy then, and
smiled in relief. "It was all because of
Maddy!" she exclaimed.

Maddy felt her own cheeks catch

fire as the crowd turned and gaped at her.

Hurrying forward, Jessica linked her arm through Maddy's. "Maddy helped me do it," she announced to everyone, her eyes shining. "*She's* not afraid of Sherry – not one bit! Isn't that right, Maddy?"

The crowd gazed at Maddy in respectful silence. Maddy swallowed. "Um . . . well . . ."

"Ooh, here comes Sherry now!" squealed a dark-haired girl. Spinning round, Maddy saw Sherry and her gang heading straight towards them, looking grim.

"Maddy's not scared, though," Jessica told everyone confidently. "*Are* you, Maddy?"

Rachel had arrived, hovering at

the edge of the group with a worried
frown. Maddy caught her eye in a
panic. This wasn't how they had
planned it at all!

"Oi, *Maddy*," called Sherry,
stopping a couple of metres away.
"C'mere – *now*!"

Maddy cringed, her heart thumping
wildly. She had never seen Sherry
so angry. Oh, what had she *done*?

Sherry put her hands on her hips.
"Ha!" she sneered. "Too scared to
even talk to me, aren't you?" The two
Jos sniggered.

"Of course she's not!" burst
out Jessica. "Go on, Maddy," she
whispered fervently. "Tell her off, just
like you helped me to!"

Caught in a nightmare, Maddy
walked slowly forward. The crowd

168

parted for her, wide-eyed. When she reached Sherry, she gulped. Sherry towered over her – she was as big as some of the secondary school girls!

But she didn't have Greykin.

Maddy stood as tall as she could. "Sherry, I – I challenge you!"

Sherry burst out laughing. "You *what*?"

"To a contest," clarified Maddy, her face burning. "To see who the better athlete is. And – and if I win, you have to leave me alone. Leave *all* of us alone, for good! Right, everyone?" she added hopefully, glancing over her shoulder. Class 5A stared back at her as if she'd lost her mind.

"A contest – yeah, right!" scoffed Sherry, crossing her arms over her chest. "Everyone knows I'd win

170

anyway. What's the point?"

"What's the matter, are you scared?" demanded Maddy.

A deadly silence fell. Sherry scowled ominously. "Scared? Of *you*?"

Maddy tried to sound calm. "Well, if you're not scared, then . . . why won't you do it?"

Sherry's face reddened, and she clenched her fists. "I am *not* scared!"

she shouted. "If you want a contest, you've got one!"

"And if I win, you'll leave us all alone from now on, right?" added Maddy, her heart thudding.

"Fine," snapped Sherry. Her eyes narrowed. "And what do *I* get, *when* I win?"

Maddy bit her lip. She hadn't thought about this.

"I know!" piped up spiky-haired Jo with a nasty grin. "Maddy will have to do whatever you say – like, *for ever*."

"Ooh, my own personal slave – brilliant!" cackled Sherry. "OK, Maddy, you're on. Afternoon break, behind the school. And you're going to wish you'd never started this!"

Maddy swallowed as the bell rang.

Paw Power

She was wishing it already.

She watched as Sherry and her gang sauntered off towards the front door, laughing and giving each other high-fives. The other children began drifting away as well, avoiding Maddy as though her insanity were catching.

Jessica looked more worshipful than ever. "Wow, Maddy," she breathed. "You must be really good at sport – she's twice your size!"

"Um . . . sort of," said Maddy weakly.

Rachel appeared at her side and squeezed her arm. "Don't worry, you'll

win!" she whispered in Maddy's
ear. "You've got magic powers,
remember? Sherry hasn't got a
chance!"

"What if they don't work, though?"
Maddy hissed back as Jessica walked
away. "What'll I do then . . . ?
Rachel!" Her voice rose to a shrill
squeak. "I'll have to be Sherry's
personal slave for ever!"

"Calm *down*," soothed Rachel. "Of
course they'll work. Why wouldn't
they?"

Maddy didn't know, but suddenly
she had an awful feeling. Grabbing
her school bag, she quickly found
her pencil case and took Greykin out.
Though the playground was deserted
by now, he remained in his ceramic
form, his small body cold and stiff.

Paw Power

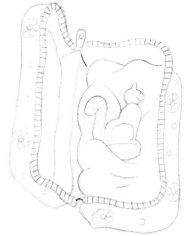

She and Rachel stared down at him. "OK, this doesn't mean anything," said Rachel finally. "You said yourself that you don't need him to be awake for your powers to work. It'll be *fine*, Maddy. Trust me!"

Maddy nodded dully, and put the little cat in her pocket. But it didn't make her feel any better.

Class 5A stood clustered around in the small yard behind the school, watching silently as Sherry paced off two giant steps and then marked the distance between them with sticks.

"There," she said, turning to

face Maddy with a sneer. "We both have to jump *that* far. And . . ." She looked around, considering. "And do twenty chin-ups from *that* branch!" she decided, pointing to the horse chestnut tree that grew in the corner. The branch was more than a metre over Maddy's head.

Maddy shrugged, trying to look unconcerned. Greykin still felt cold

and stiff in her pocket. "There should be three things," she said. "What else?"

"Maddy gets to choose the last one," put in Rachel. "It's only fair, Sherry."

Sherry smirked and crossed her arms over her chest. "Fine. Go ahead."

Let's see who can climb the highest, Maddy started to say – and then stopped, remembering how awkward climbing down again had been! "A race," she said. "From the wall to the end of the yard."

Running wasn't really a cat skill – not like jumping and climbing were – but Maddy still ran much faster than usual when she had her cat powers. If she still had them, that was. Her

177

palms felt clammy, and she wiped
them on her trousers.

"Easy-peasy!" sang Sherry, flipping
back her dark blonde hair. "Come on,
then – jumping first. *I'll* go." Striding
across to the stick that marked the
starting line, Sherry crouched down.
Her forehead creased as she eyed up
the second stick, preparing to leap.

Cat, thought Maddy, closing her
eyes. *Cat, cat, cat* . . .

"Hey, you have to watch!" shouted
Sherry.

Maddy's eyes flew open. Sherry
was standing up, scowling at her.
"What's the matter?" she taunted.
"Too scared to watch me beat you?"

"Of course not!" said Maddy,
flushing. Oh, *where* were her cat
powers? She chewed her lip nervously

178

as Sherry crouched down again.

"Ready . . . steady . . . *go!*" chanted
the two Jos.

Sherry sprang into the air. *Thump!*
She landed a few centimetres away
from the second stick, and bobbed
up with a triumphant leer. "Ha! Beat
that!"

Cat, cat, cat, thought Maddy
desperately. *Oh, where* are *you? Cat,
cat* . . . And then, to her immense
relief, she felt the familiar tingling
flow through her. Her powers had
come back!

"OK," she said with a grin. She
strolled over to the first stick. "But
let me just get this straight. Is it *that*
stick I'm supposed to jump to?" she
asked, pointing. Before Sherry could
reply, Maddy leaped, feeling the wind

blowing through her hair.

Whoomp!

"Or this one?" she finished innocently, turning round and pointing to a twig at her feet.

Sherry and the rest of 5A stood three metres behind her, their mouths hanging open like a group of dumbstruck fish. Only Rachel was smiling widely. She gave Maddy a thumbs-up.

"You won!" gasped Jessica,

recovering. "Maddy, that was brilliant!"

"She – she must have cheated," sputtered Sherry. "No way could she have really jumped that far!"

"How could she have cheated?" said Rachel. "We all saw it."

"Yeah, Sherry, she won fair and square," put in a boy called Peter.

Unexpectedly, Maddy felt a pang of conscience. Sherry was right – she *had* cheated. She cleared her throat.

"Um . . . shall we do chin-ups now?"

Chattering excitedly, the class trooped after her as she crossed the yard to the horse chestnut tree. Bounding upwards, Maddy grabbed the branch and performed twenty chin-ups easily, cat strength flowing through her arms. The class cheered.

Sherry only managed twelve before dropping to the ground with an angry

huff. After Maddy had won the race as well – streaking past to touch the fence before Sherry had even gone halfway – the larger girl's face turned bright red.

"She *is* cheating!" she insisted, stamping her foot. "I don't know how, but she is!"

"Don't be a sore loser, Sherry," said Rachel.

"Yeah," said someone else. "Maddy won, that's all – and now you've got to leave everyone alone like you promised."

5A echoed their agreement.

"Not when she *cheated* I don't," snarled Sherry.

"No one cheated," said a boy named Tom. "Maddy's just better than you, that's all."

183

Chapter Seven

"Yeah, Maddy's miles better!" laughed Jessica. "Right, Maddy?"

"Er . . ." Maddy trailed off as guilt flushed hotly through her. Somehow, beating Sherry wasn't quite as much fun as she'd imagined.

Sherry looked like a cornered rat. "She is *not* better than me!" she shouted. Glancing around wildly, she suddenly leaped onto the grey drainpipe that snaked up the side of the school building.

"I bet you can't climb *this*, Maddy," she called. And as 5A watched in startled silence, Sherry started climbing the wall, pulling herself up by her hands and feet.

184

Chapter Eight

Higher and higher Sherry went, until she was almost at the second floor. Maddy stared up at her in horror. "Sherry, stop!" she called as loudly as she dared, hoping that there weren't any teachers nearby. "You could fall!"

But Sherry kept going,
grimly pulling herself up
the side of the building.
When she was halfway
up, she paused and peered
down. All at once Maddy
saw her face turn pale.
She gave a squeaking
noise, and gripped the
drainpipe hard with her
hands and feet.

Long moments passed.
Sherry stayed where she
was, not moving. 5A
glanced worriedly at
each other.

"She's stuck," said Jessica, biting
her fingernail.

"Look!" gasped Rachel, pointing.

Gazing upwards, Maddy caught her

breath. Sherry was slipping! Though clutching the drainpipe for all she was worth, she was starting to lose her grip, the smooth pipe sliding through her fingers. As Maddy watched, Sherry dropped jerkily by several centimetres.

"Argh!" she cried.

"Someone's got to climb up and hold onto her!" burst out pointy-faced Jo, her sharp features pale. "She'll fall otherwise."

"Maddy! *You* could do it!" said Rachel, gripping her arm.

Maddy nodded quickly. With her cat powers, she knew she could easily scale the drainpipe and hold Sherry in place until help came. "OK," she said. "You go and get a teacher!"

She hurried over to the wall as

187

Rachel raced off. Suddenly she felt
a sharp claw jabbing her trousers.
Greykin!

She slipped her hand in her pocket.
The little cat squirmed into her
sleeve and up her arm. "You must be
careful!" he hissed urgently from her
shoulder, hidden by her long hair.
"There's no *ka* left – you're on your
own!"

Maddy's hands turned to ice. "No
ka? But—"

Paw Power

"No, that's why I've stayed ceramic!" Greykin's tail swished fretfully from side to side. "When your mother went into your room to put your laundry away this morning, she looked at the other two cats again – and she didn't put them back together afterwards. There's barely enough *ka* left to keep *me* going now, much less to power you any more!"

"Maddy, what are you waiting for?" called someone. "You have to hurry!"

"I—" Maddy's throat was dry. 5A were staring at her, the same expectant expression on all their faces. They knew she could climb the drainpipe; hadn't she just proved what a great athlete she was? Only she *wasn't*, and she was scared of heights!

Sherry gave a
strangled shriek as
she slipped again,
scrabbling to hang
on with her knees.
Maddy felt dizzy,
looking upwards
. . . and then she
decided. Pushing
all thoughts of being
scared to the back of
her mind, she gripped
the drainpipe with
trembling hands and
started to climb.
"That's it,"
whispered Greykin,
balancing on her
shoulder. "Easy does it."
Maddy's heart was

190

thumping so wildly that she thought it might burst from her chest. But to her surprise, the drainpipe wasn't difficult to scale. Her legs were strong from doing ballet, and she was so light that she could pull herself up easily.

Just don't look down! she thought, gulping hard. She stared fervently at her hands as she pulled herself up bit by bit.

In what seemed like no time at all, Maddy had reached Sherry's feet. She held onto a windowsill to her left, bracing herself, and grabbed Sherry's legs with her other arm. She could hear Sherry crying, and her own fear faded.

"It's all right, Sherry," she said gently. "Don't cry, I've got you."

Sherry peered down at Maddy, her face smudged and tear-stained.

Chapter Eight

"You – you won't tell the others how scared I am, will you?" she choked out. "Please!"

Maddy hesitated. She thought the others probably already knew, to be honest.

"*Please*," implored Sherry, her voice cracking. "I'll do anything!"

Greykin whispered something in Maddy's ear, and Maddy felt a smile spread over her face. "OK," she said. "I won't tell – but only if you keep your promise and leave everyone alone from now on."

Sherry gulped, and then nodded hard. "I – I promise!"

Down below, Rachel had just come running up with two teachers. As one of them propped a ladder up beside the drainpipe and started to climb,

Sherry whispered, "But, Maddy . . . how *did* you win?"

Maddy could feel Greykin nestled under the shoulder of her jumper, his small weight warm and comforting. "I don't know," she smiled. "Magic, I suppose."

Paw Power

That night Maddy sat at her desk, her
heart as heavy as a stone. "Don't be
sad," murmured Greykin, rubbing
against her finger. His thick blue-grey
fur was velvet-soft. "You'll meet one
of the others soon enough."

"I know, but . . . oh, *Greykin*,"
choked out Maddy. She felt as if she
had only just found him, and now it
was time to say goodbye!

"Now, now. You'll be too busy with your detention to even notice I'm gone," said Greykin with a small smile.

Both Maddy and Sherry had received a week's detention for climbing the drainpipe – though Sherry had unexpectedly taken all the blame, explaining that Maddy was only trying to help. Even so, Maddy's parents had been cross that she'd behaved so recklessly . . . though she had a feeling that they were proud of her, as well.

"I could *never* be that busy," Maddy said. The words felt strangled in her throat. She stroked Greykin's silky back. "Will – will I ever see you again?"

"Of course!" Standing on his

196

haunches, Greykin clutched Maddy's finger in his tiny paws and gave it a shake. "We've bonded with you, the three of us – that means you'll have us around for a good long time to come. Agreed?"

Maddy tried to smile, though all she really wanted was Greykin *now*. "Agreed," she said softly. Lifting Greykin up, she nuzzled him to her damp cheek.

197

He gave a rumbling purr, rubbing his head against her tears. "You know, Maddy Lloyd," he said softly, "I do believe that you're my favourite of all the humans I've ever had. And you're a lot braver than you thought you were, aren't you?"

"I suppose," mumbled Maddy. Somehow it didn't seem to matter very much.

She cuddled the little cat for a long time. Finally she knew she could put the moment off no longer, and she set him down on her desk. "*Au revoir*," said Greykin, his golden eyes gleaming. "We shall meet again soon, Maddy."

Maddy nodded, her heart too full to speak.

Greykin strolled across the desk

198

to the other two cats, who sat locked
together in their painted embrace. He
stood very still, positioning himself so
that his grey tail was wrapped around
the black one, and his grey paw linked
with the tabby's.

Slowly his living fur faded, and
cold, hard ceramic took its place.

Maddy sat looking at him for a

long time. What she had learned about herself *did* matter, she realized suddenly. Greykin had shown her that she wasn't such a coward after all – she had powers of her own, with or without magic.

Unconsciously, Maddy sat up a bit straighter. "Goodbye for now, Greykin," she whispered, touching his face. "And thank you."

Paw Power

Her gaze went to the other two cats: the slender black one, and the long-haired tabby with the laughing eyes. What would they be like when she met them?

Despite the knot of sorrow in her throat, Maddy felt a flutter of anticipation. She smiled. "And hello to the two of you, when the time comes. I can hardly wait!"

THE END

Don't miss Maddy's next adventure!
Pocket Cats: Shadow Magic

Maddy can't wait to get to know Nibs, the second Pocket Cat to come to life! But there's a problem to be solved, and it doesn't take long for Maddy and Nibs to figure out who needs their help. Maddy's cousin Chloe is having trouble settling into her new school; she's so miserable that she's decided to run away. Can Maddy and Nibs use their Shadow Magic to stop her?